THE GIFT OF

Self - Love

30 day challenge
A guided JOURNAL to help you chart
self-care and personal growth

"To those embracing the journey of self-discovery and growth—
may these 30 days inspire you to unlock your inner strength and
find joy in every step forward."

Mirabilia Darline

TH IS

moment in time happiness can be found.

This journal belongs to _____

♥

hello

Developing habits for self-love is like trying to train a cat —tricky, but totally worth it! It's more than just indulging in fleeting moments of joy; it's about shaking up your daily routine and putting in the effort to become the person you truly want to be. This 30-day journal challenge is your chance to add some spice to your daily grind and put yourself first for a change.

Remember, your life isn't just about going through the motions—you've got the potential to thrive, shine, and find real happiness. So, believe in yourself, grab that pen, and let's make this happen!

Mirabilia Darline

P.S. I love you, and I believe in you. Please share your progress on my Facebook page—your journey will inspire me and others.

 Day 1 ♥

Cook your fa orite meal.

WHAT DID YOU COOK AND HOW DID IT TURN OUT.

BEING SELFLESS DOES WONDERS FOR THE SPIRIT.

 **Day 2** ♥

Get some sunlight.

WHAT DID YOU DO TO ACCOMPLISH THIS?

_____

_____

_____

_____

_____

_____

_____

_____

_____

_____

_____

_____

_____

_____

_____

_____

_____

_____

_____

_____

_____

_____

_____

_____

_____

_____

_____

Be aware of what you
are saying, while you
are saying it..

♥

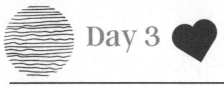

Day 3 ♥

Write out one goal.

ARE YOU USING A PEN OR PENCIL?

♥

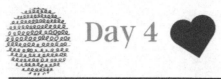

Day 4 ♥

Practice meditation.

DID YOU DO THIS ALONE OR WITH A FRIEND?

_____

_____

_____

_____

_____

_____

_____

_____

_____

_____

_____

_____

_____

_____

_____

_____

_____

_____

_____

_____

_____

_____

_____

**TURN YOUR COMPLAINTS
INTO A POSITIVE EXPERIENCE.**

Day 5 ♥

Read a book.

WAS IT A NEW TITLE OR AN OLD FAVORITE?

_____
_____
_____
_____
_____
_____
_____
_____
_____
_____
_____
_____
_____
_____
_____
_____
_____
_____
_____
_____
_____
_____
_____
_____
_____
_____

DO YOUR BEST TO BE PART OF THE
SOLUTION AND NOT THE PROBLEM.

 **Day 6** ♥

Drink more water.

DID YOU GULP OR SIP?

♥

WHEN YOU DO SOMETHING KIND FOR SOMEONE, KEEP IT TO
YOURSELF AND SAVOR THE ABUNDANT JOY OF THE ACT.

 Day 7 ♥

Listen to a fa orite song.

YOU CAN LIST MORE THAN ONE.

_____
_____
_____
_____
_____
_____
_____
_____
_____
_____
_____
_____
_____
_____
_____
_____
_____
_____
_____
_____
_____
_____
_____

**LIFE ISN'T THE END RESULT—IT IS EVERYTHING
IN BETWEEN THE BEGINNING AND THE END.**

Day 8 ♥

Be grateful!

THIS LIST WILL BE AMAZING.

Tic Tac Toe!

 Day 9 ♥

Learn a new skill.

NO SWEAT INTENDED.

WITHOUT MISTAKES THERE WOULD BE NO REASON FOR CHANGE.

Day 10 ♥

Go to bed earlier.

SAVE THIS ONE FOR THE WEEKEND TO GET A LONGER REST.

WHEN WE MAKE A MOUNTAIN OVER A MOLE HILL THE TASK
IS ACCOMPANIED BY CHAOS, CONFUSION AND STRESS.

Day 11 ♥

Try a DIY project.

HUM! PULL ONE OFF THAT TO DO LIST.

SUCCESS WILL NOT COME WITHOUT ENTHUSIASM.

 # Day 12 ♥

Watch the sunset.

DO IT WITH A SMILE.

♥

Life is not a dress rehearsal
for some later date.

Day 13 ♥

Make a gratitude journal.

IT DOESN'T HAVE TO BE FANCY.

_____

_____

_____

_____

_____

_____

_____

_____

_____

_____

_____

_____

_____

_____

_____

_____

_____

_____

_____

_____

_____

_____

_____

_____

_____

_____

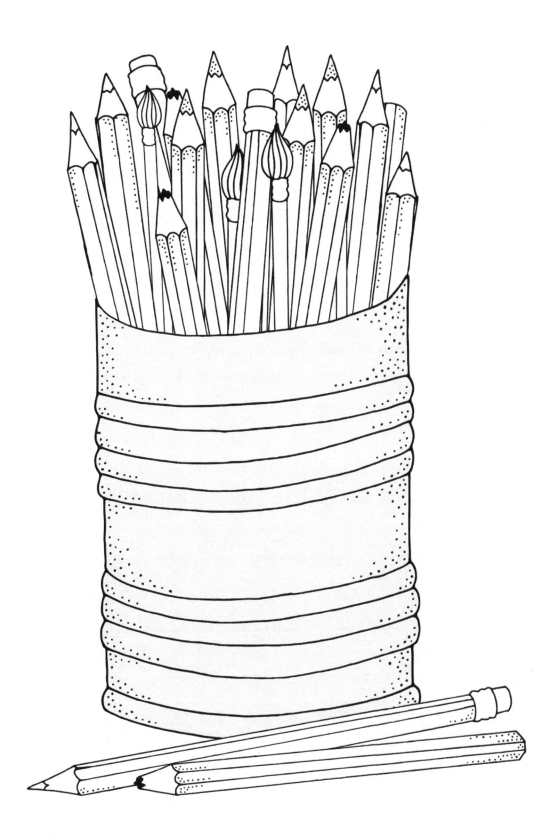

Day 14 ♥

Start a new hobby.

OR REKINDLE AN OLD ONE.

A CALM MIND IS RESOURCEFUL.

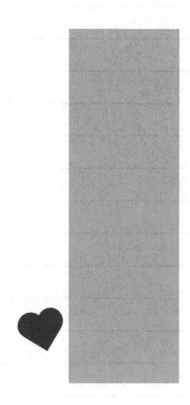

EVERYONE MAKES MISTAKES.

 **Day 15** ♥

Go for a walk in nature.

IT'S ALL AROUND US.

MINDFULNESS, IS SIMPLE, BUT NOT NECESSARILY AN EASY PROCESS.

Day 16 ♥

Organize a closet.

EENIE MEENIE MINEY MO

THERE CAN BE AN INHERENT SATISFACTION IN THE PROCESS OF SHARING.

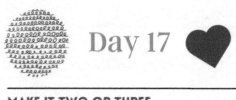 Day 17 ♥

Gi e yourself a facial.

MAKE IT TWO OR THREE.

Instead of being overwhelmed by a situation, take a moment and look for the humor.

♥

Day 18 ♥

Stretch all your muscles.

A GOOD WAY TO START THE DAY.

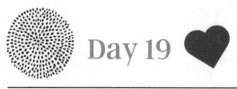

Day 19 ♥

Explore a new city.

DAY TRIPS ARE NICE.

_____

_____

_____

_____

_____

_____

_____

_____

_____

_____

_____

_____

_____

_____

_____

_____

_____

_____

_____

_____

_____

_____

_____

_____

Quiet your mind and settle your heart.

 **Day 20** *Stay away from social media for a day.*

YOUR FINGERS WILL THANK YOU.

LISTENING WILL HELP PRODUCE
GOOD RESULTS IN RELATIONSHIPS.

Day 21 ♥

Watch your fa orite mo ie.

FLAVORED POPCORN CAN BE NICE.

_____

_____

_____

_____

_____

_____

_____

_____

_____

_____

_____

_____

_____

_____

_____

_____

_____

_____

_____

_____

_____

_____

IF YOU FOCUS ON ONLY THAT WHICH IS WRONG, YOU
WILL ROB YOURSELF OF THE QUALITY MOMENTS OF LIFE.

Day 22 ♥

Go on a solo date.

OOH LA LA!

_____

_____

_____

_____

_____

_____

_____

_____

_____

_____

_____

_____

_____

_____

_____

_____

_____

_____

_____

_____

_____

_____

_____

_____

_____

We could not exist without change.

♥

Day 23

Get some sunlight.

OUTSIDE RELAXATION IS A PLUS.

_____

_____

_____

_____

_____

_____

_____

_____

_____

_____

_____

_____

_____

_____

_____

_____

_____

_____

_____

_____

_____

Day 24 ♥

Take a nice bubble bath.

DITCH THE SHOWER CAP.

Have wisdom or the courage
to ask questions.

Day 25

Gi e yourself a break.

WHAT DOES THIS LOOK LIKE ?

_____

_____

_____

_____

_____

_____

_____

_____

_____

_____

_____

_____

_____

_____

_____

_____

_____

_____

_____

_____

_____

_____

Day 26 ♥

Eat a nutrious breakfast.

YUM! YUM!

Give others the joy
of being right.

♥

Day 27 ♥

Eat a vegetarian meal.

GREENS, REDS AND YELLOWS, OH MY!

BE ♥

the one that others
describe as "always
ethical."

Day 28 ♥

Make your fa orite drink.

WOW! ONE LUMP OR TWO?

If we hold onto anger
we will exhaust our mind.

Day 29 ♥

Treat yourself to something new.

CAREFUL THIS COULD BECOME A HABIT.

Find something positive
to focus on.

♥

Day 30 ♥

Dance like no one is watching.

FREE STYLE

DELIBERATE PRACTICE OF PATIENCE ENHANCES THE QUALITY OF THE HEART.

Day 31 ♥

Visit a place in your city where you ha e ne er been before.

The storm isn't bad its
how you weather it.

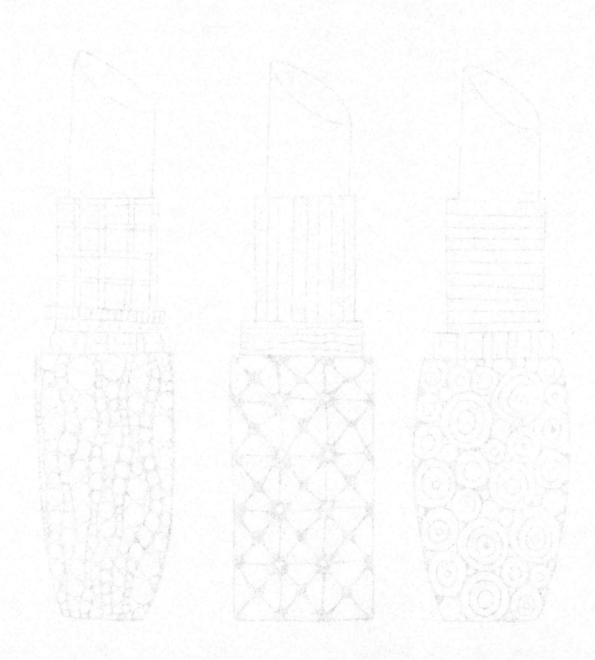

Coloring Test Page

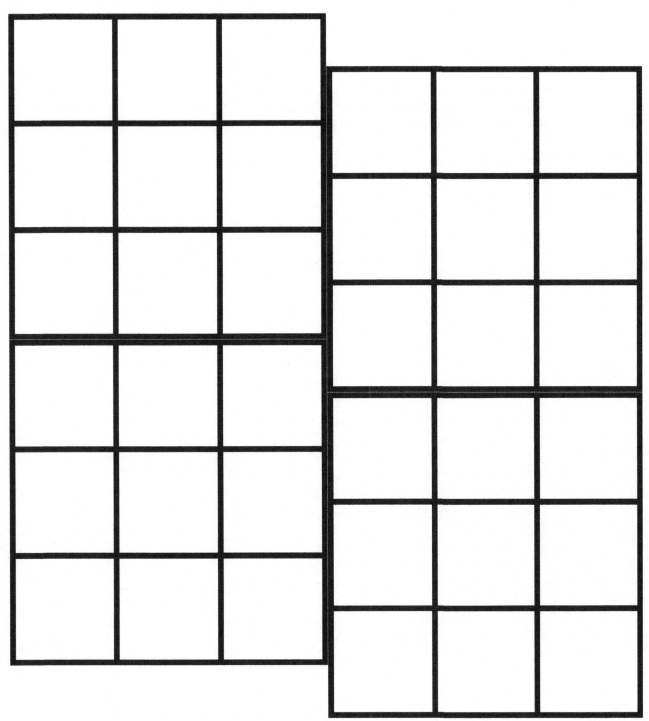

This journal is like your well-meaning but slightly clueless friend who's great with advice but not a doctor. It's here to help you build positive habits and boost your well-being, but it's not a replacement for professional medical advice or treatment. If you're dealing with a health issue or need treatment, please consult an actual healthcare professional, not just this journal. The author and publishers aren't liable if you try to use this journal to diagnose yourself or solve your problems—though we're sure it'll make you smile along the way!

list & notes

_____
_____
_____
_____
_____
_____
_____
_____
_____
_____
_____
_____
_____
_____
_____

Made in United States
Orlando, FL
20 November 2024